The Sleepover Club
at Frankie's

A BOYFRIEND
FOR BROWN OWL

by Rose Impey

Collins

An imprint of HarperCollins*Publishers*

The Sleepover Club ® is a
registered trademark of HarperCollins*Publishers* Ltd

First published in Great Britain by Collins in 1997
This edition published in Great Britain by Collins in 2003
Collins is an imprint of HarperCollins*Publishers* Ltd
77-85 Fulham Palace Road, Hammersmith,
London, W6 8JB

The HarperCollins*Children'sBooks* website address is:
www.harpercollinschildrensbooks.co.uk

4

Text copyright © Rose Impey 1997

ISBN 0 00 716940 X

The Sleepover Club

Have you been invited to all these sleepovers?

You are invited to a sleepover at Frankie's.

It's at Frankie's house — obviously!
17, The Ridgeway
Melford Road
Cuddington
Leicester

It's on Saturday 21 September.
So be there or be square!

Come at 4 o'clock for the wedding of the year
— Fliss and Lyndz! Don't forget your wedding
clothes. The reception will be at 5 o'clock,
followed by sleepover and usual mad times.

from,
Francesca Theresa Thomas

SLEEPOVER KIT LIST

1. Sleeping bag
2. Pillow
3. Pyjamas or a nightdress, but they're draughty and fly up and show your bottom when you do gymnastics
4. Slippers
5. Toothbrush, toothpaste, soap etc
6. Towel
7. Teddy
8. A creepy story
9. Food for a midnight feast, chocolate, crisps, sweeties, biscuits and any other yummy foods you can bring.
10. A torch.
11. Hairbrush
12. Hair things like a bobble or hairband, if you need them
13. Clean knickers and socks. And a smelly bag for old ones!
14. Sleepover diary

For the wedding:
15. Wedding clothes
16. Camera
17. Confetti

CHAPTER ONE

Well, come in, if you're coming in. And sit down. This time we're in deep trouble. This time we could be in doom for ever. And this time it was *not* my idea. Uh-oh! There's the phone.

"Frankie! It's for you."

"Coming, Mum."

You'd better come down and listen in. I've got a feeling this could be *bad* news.

"Hello?"

"Frankie, is that you?"

"No, it's Betty Boop."

"Look, be serious for once. Has Brown Owl been round to your house?"

"No! Why?"

"She's been here already, so you'd better look out."

"What happened? Go on, tell me the worst."

"I can't, my mum's coming. I've been grounded and that includes the phone."

"Oh, help, Kenny! I think she's at the door now. What should I do?"

"Hide. Run away. Emigrate. But disappear!"

Come on. 5-4-3-2-1, let's get gone! Upstairs, quick!

Right, close that door. On second thoughts, lock it, we don't want to be disturbed. This is seriously serious. What do you think she'll tell them? Oh, p-lease, not everything! I mean, we haven't done anything terrible. It's not as if we *meant* to wreck the supermarket. We were just trying to be helpful, which is what she's always telling us Brownies are supposed to be.

I blame Rosie. None of this would have happened if we hadn't let her join the Sleepover Club. That was the start of it all. Oh, flipping Ada, as my grandma says, pull up a pew. I suppose I'd better tell you exactly what happened.

To begin with there were just the four of us.

There was me, Francesca Thomas. But you can call me Frankie.

And there was Laura McKenzie. We call her Kenny. She's my best friend. That doesn't mean we never fall out – we argue at least once a day – but we always make it up.

And Fliss. Her real name's Felicity Sidebotham, but please don't bother with the jokes, she's heard them all before. And, as everybody knows, Fliss doesn't have much of a sense of humour.

And Lyndsey Collins. Now *she* does. Lyndz is a great laugh.

So that's how it *used* to be.

Now there's Rosie as well, which, in case you can't count, makes five.

Rosie's only recently moved round here; she doesn't know many people yet, so we thought we'd be friendly. OK, we were curious as well. She'd moved into that big house at the end of Welby Drive, the one with the massive garden with an orchard, so we were expecting someone really posh. But Rosie is not posh. Up to now we haven't been inside, but we're working on it.

It was Lyndsey who suggested we let Rosie sit with us in class and hang around with us at dinner, which was cool with us, but then, the next thing, she said, "I think we should let Rosie join the Sleepover Club."

I said, "What for?" as if I needed to ask.

"Well, I feel sorry for her; she's got no

friends." Lyndz is the sort of person that would rescue a fly if it fell in a puddle.

"That's not our problem," said Fliss. "Anyway it would make five and five's an odd number and odd numbers never work." Fliss likes everything to be tidy. She even lifts hairs off your cardigan while she's talking to you.

But for once I agreed with her. "We don't really know her, do we? She might be a drip. She might be a scaredy cat. She might be really boring."

"She's not," said Lyndz. "She passed the test, didn't she?"

I suppose she did. We wouldn't even have let her hang around with us at school otherwise. We do these naughty things: you know, like screwing up paper pellets and stuffing them down the back of the art cupboard to feed Muriel, our pretend pet monster. Sometimes we tie one of us to a tree behind the mobile classroom, then knock on the door and run away. If you want to be in the gang you have to do a dare and get sent to Mrs Poole's office. We dared Rosie to take a bite out of a biscuit in the teachers' tin on the staff-room table and then put it back. She ate half the biscuit, so we had to let her join. But there's something about her I'm still not sure about.

"Well, I don't care who joins," said Kenny, "as long as we have a laugh."

"But she doesn't laugh, that's the trouble," I said. "She's a bit of a sad case, really."

"That's because her dad's left," said Lyndz.

"So's mine," said Fliss.

"Yes, but you've got another one," Kenny pointed out.

"Andy is not my dad," Fliss insisted.

We argued for ages until Fliss said, "Let's stop bickering and have a vote and settle it once and for all." She can be so bossy sometimes. "Those in favour."

Lyndz and Kenny put up their hands.

"Those against."

Me and Fliss put up ours.

"Oh, well, that really settles it," I said. "Now what do we do?"

Well, we didn't do anything, until the following week when we were all at Brownies. We were sitting on the wall outside, waiting for Kenny's dad to pick us up. We were talking about our next sleepover, which was at my house the following weekend. Just then Rosie came over, because she's started Brownies too.

"I've got these really cute Forever Friends jimjams," Fliss was telling us. "You'll see them at the sleepover on Saturday."

"What's that?" asked Rosie.

Suddenly everyone went quiet. Kenny started to whistle, which she always does when she's nervous. I looked at my feet, which are pretty fascinating. No, really, they are, because they're the biggest feet you've ever seen. I take size sixes already. Of course I'm tall for my age and, as my mum says, if I didn't have big feet I'd be for ever falling over. Fliss sucked her cheeks in, which is a silly habit and makes her look like a gerbil. Then, out of the blue, we all heard Lyndz say, "Oh, it's our Sleepover Club. It's at Frankie's house on Friday. Do you want to come?"

After Rosie had gone, Fliss turned on her and said, "Why did you say that?"

But she needn't have asked. We all said together, "*Because she felt sorry for her!*"

So that was it. Thanks to big-hearted Lyndsey, with a mouth to match, we now had five in the Sleepover Club.

CHAPTER TWO

Of course that was only part of it. The other person I blame is Fliss. If she wasn't so potty about weddings, we definitely wouldn't be in this mess now. And I wouldn't be sitting here, hiding in my bedroom from Brown Owl.

Fliss is so potty about weddings that she even marries her toys. Whenever you go round to her house, there's a rabbit in a wedding dress or a teddy wearing a veil or a Barbie getting married to a My Little Pony. She reads a bit out of the Bible, plays a tune on the keyboard and then she says, "And now you may kiss the bride." Then they get to sit together on a shelf in their wedding clothes living happily ever after.

That's how she came up with her bright idea. "Why don't we have a wedding at our next sleepover?" she said, dead excited.

"*A wedding*?" I said.

"Yeah. I could be the bride, and you could be the groom."

"Why me?"

"Because you've got a boy's name."

"So's Kenny."

"You're the tallest. Kenny can be bridesmaid. You'll have to wear a dress, though," she told Kenny, "you can't wear your soccer strip."

I said, "Dream on!"

Kenny grinned and sat there shaking her head. Kenny lives and dies in her football top. She's devoted to Leicester City football team and just about everything she wears has got The Fox's logo on it. Me and Kenny have been friends since playschool and I have never seen her in a frilly frock.

"Anyway," I said, "you can forget it. I'm not marrying anybody."

"I'll marry you," Lyndz said.

"Brillo," said Fliss and gave Lyndz a hug.

So we worked it all out: Kenny would be best man and I'd be the vicar. I'd borrow a white cotton nightie of my mum's and Fliss's Bible and an old pair of Dad's glasses. All my toys and Pepsi, our dog, would be the guests and we'd do it out in the garden. All we were short of was a bridesmaid, so, at the time, it seemed quite lucky that Rosie joined the Sleepover Club when she did.

Lyndz has an excellent set of dressing-up clothes that used to be her mum's. She brought Fliss an old wedding dress and a net curtain for a veil; she found a soldier's outfit for herself to wear, and painted on a moustache. There was a pink fairy dress that Rosie wore, and Kenny wore her soccer strip with a jacket over the top.

We all had to hum the "Here comes the bride" tune and then Lyndz and Fliss walked down my garden path through the arch where the roses used to grow, before Pepsi dug them up. Arm in arm.

I started off, "We are gathered here," and then I rambled on till everyone started to look bored. I didn't say the bit about "And now you may kiss the bride" because Lyndz had made me promise to leave it out. But we did the bit where they exchange rings. And then we took lots of photos. Pepsi got too excited and kept running off with the other guests in her mouth, so in the end we had to lock her in the house.

At last we got to the best bit: the food. We had veggie hot dogs, popcorn, crisp-

and-banana sandwiches, marshmallows, lemon jelly, and chocolate fudge cake. Sometimes, when we've finished, we get a big salad bowl and mix all the leftovers together, hot dogs, crisps, jelly, the lot, and stir it up until it looks like a dog's dinner. We call it Nappy's Brains. We call it that because there's a boy called Nathan, who lives next door to me, who we call Nappyhead, because he's really stupid. But don't let me get started on that subject or I'll never finish this story.

Usually we dare someone to eat it. I looked round and chose Kenny.

"I dare you," I said to her.

"I double dare you," she said to me.

"I triple dare you," I said to her.

"Oh, that's not fair," said Lyndz. "It's always Kenny has to do it."

"All right, I dare Rosie," I said.

Everyone went quiet because they thought it was mean to dare Rosie when she was still new. But I don't see what difference that makes. Anyway she picked up the spoon and ate two heaped spoonfuls. We all collapsed on the floor gagging and pretending to be sick, but she just rolled her eyes and looked at us as if we were really weird. So that was another test she'd passed.

After that it was time to go to bed. I've got quite a big bedroom with a bed *and* a set of bunks in it. And we've got a camp bed. So, when the sleepover's at mine, all four of us can fit in.

You see, I'm an only child, which is a very sore point in my house. I've just about given up trying to persuade my parents to have another baby, but I still don't like it. They don't seem to realise what a disadvantage it is to grow up an only child. So I think the least they can do is make it up to me by letting me have my friends round to stay whenever I want, which they usually do. So that's pretty coo-el.

But there wasn't a bed for Rosie, so Kenny and I had to share my bed. This seemed like a great idea until she got the giggles and the fidgets, which always happens with Kenny. She also has the most freezing feet in the world!

Because Rosie is new, she doesn't have a sleepover kit like the rest of us, so Felicity showed her what she needed to get. We all have a bag and in it is:

1. Sleeping bag
2. Pillow
3. Pyjamas or a nightdress, but they're draughty and fly up and show your bottom when you do gymnastics
4. Slippers
5. Toothbrush, toothpaste, soap etc
6. Towel
7. Teddy
8. A creepy story

9. Food for a midnight feast: chocolate, crisps, sweeties, biscuits and any other yummy foods you can bring.
10. A torch
11. Hairbrush
12. Hair things like a bobble or hairband, if you need them
13. Clean knickers and socks. And a smelly bag for old ones!
14. Sleepover diary

For the wedding:
15. Wedding clothes
16. Camera
17. Confetti

We all keep a diary. Sometimes we read each other bits out of them, but they are *absolutely private*, on pain of death! We would never look in each other's without permission. We write all our secret secrets in them. If you haven't got any secrets, you can make them up. At least, that's what I do.

I wrote in mine: *When I grow up I don't want to be a pop star any more. I want to drive a taxi.*

I went in a taxi for the first time last week when we went to London. It was class.

Kenny was writing loads in hers, all about what she'd learned about how babies are made. She read it out to us. Kenny's going to be a doctor, like her dad, when she grows up. She says you have to be really tough to be a doctor. She loves anything with blood in it. And she knows all about babies and things. She wrote: *I'm not going to have a baby, though. And I'm not getting married. I shall be far too busy saving lives.*

Felicity started to giggle. "I am," she said. "I'm going to marry Ryan Scott and have lots of children and run a playgroup."

Ryan Scott is a boy in our class. Kenny made a being-sick noise.

I said, "He's the saddest thing on earth."

"Boys smell," said Lyndz, wrinkling her nose. And Lyndz has four brothers, so she should know.

"How do you like boys?" I asked Rosie.

"In a sandwich," she said, "with tomato ketchup and chips on the side."

"Yeah! good one," I said.

Suddenly thinking about chips made us all feel hungry. It wasn't midnight yet, but we decided to have our midnight feast. I sneaked downstairs to get a big bowl and we put everything in it. There was fizzy rock, Black Jacks, Fruit Salads, chewy dinosaurs, jelly babies, a Snickers bar, and a bag of cheese and onion crisps. We passed it round and started talking about Brownies.

"It's no fun any more," said Kenny.

It's true. It used to be supercool, but it's boring these days.

"Brown Owl's always in a razz."

"She used to be really nice," said Lyndz.

"It's because she's fallen out with her boyfriend," said Fliss. "Auntie Jill told me." Fliss's Auntie Jill is Snowy Owl, that's how she knows so much. "She told my mum Brown Owl might give up running Brownies because she just doesn't feel interested in anything any more."

"That's a shame," said Lyndsey. "I feel—"

"*Really sorry for her!*" we all chimed in.

"Well, I do! It's horrid when somebody gets dumped."

"You should see my mum," said Rosie. "Since my dad left, she looks much happier."

But you could tell by the way she said it that Rosie wasn't happy. We knew she was missing her dad, but we didn't know what to say to cheer her up.

It was half past twelve and there was

nothing left to eat. We were lying in the dark with our torches on, starting to get dozy. We were trying hard to stay awake. After all, the whole idea of sleepover is *not* to go to sleep.

Lyndz is always the first to drop off. We could hear her sucking her thumb. Then Fliss started sniffing, which she always does, so Kenny and I played pass the sniff. We do it at school in silent reading, it drives Mrs Weaver mad. Then Rosie joined in, which made me and Kenny giggle. Suddenly Kenny sat up in bed. She'd had this idea.

"Why don't we find her a *new* boyfriend?" she said.

"Who?" said Rosie.

"Brown Owl, of course."

"How would we do that?" I said. I meant, where would you look? There isn't exactly a shop to go to.

"Well, there must be someone out there," said Kenny.

"Mmm," Rosie agreed.

I was just dropping off, which is the time when I get most of my brilliant ideas. "What about Dishy Dave?" I said, yawning.

"Who's Dishy Dave?" said Rosie.

But I was too tired to explain. "Tell you … in the… morn… ing," I said, and fell asleep.

CHAPTER THREE

We usually wake up in the opposite order to the way we go to sleep. Lyndz is always awake first and once *she's* awake, everyone's awake. She's the noisiest person alive. She was sleeping on the camp bed and every time she moved, it squeaked. And when she leant over to reach for her sleepover bag, the camp bed collapsed at one end and catapulted her out on the floor.

So she woke us all up squealing and giggling. The next thing, she'd got the hiccups. When Lyndz gets hiccups, she really gets hiccups. She could get in the *Guinness Book of Records* for hiccups.

We've tried all sorts of ways of curing her of them: a cold key down her back, giving her a fright, standing on her head – No, not us standing on her head! – wet flannels, pinching her nose, making her sing "God Save the Queen" backwards. But best of all is pressing down hard with your thumbs on the palm of her hand, while she holds her breath.

But the minute you wake up in the morning is not a time when your brain is working well. So it took a bit longer than usual, and the longer the hiccups went on, the pinker Lyndz's face got and the more she hiccuped. In the end I managed it with my magic thumbs, but some people are never grateful.

"That really hurt," she complained, rubbing her hand.

"Oh, tell me about it," I said. I thought my thumbs would never recover. Then I tripped over the camp bed, which folded under me, so I ended up on the floor too.

Lyndz made the mistake of laughing. OK, I thought, *payback time*! And I picked up Stanley, who is my toughest bear.

Teddy fights are one of our favourite things. Sometimes we use pillows, but the best fights are with squishy-poos. A squishy-poo is a sleeping bag filled with clothes and things, which you whack each other with while balancing on a bed. That's one of our International Gladiator events. But you need plenty of room for that.

When it's a teddy fight, Stanley always wins because he's stuffed really hard and he's quite big. You can see the other bears tremble when they see him coming. Stanley is unbeatable.

I could see Rosie watching us again, thinking *definitely weird*. But she'll get used to us in time. Then my dad came in, so we had to stop.

"When you've quite finished the demolition job, it's time for breakfast," he said.

While we were getting ready, Rosie said, "Now tell me who Dishy Dave is."

"You know, he's the new caretaker at school," said Fliss, butting in before I could speak. "Dave's great."

He is great. He used to drive a mobile library van before he came to our school. He's quite young and we all like him because he doesn't tell us off. He's really nice to the infants. Sometimes, if they offer him a cup of tea, he sits down in the home corner with a crown on his head and pretends to be Prince Charles. He's a good laugh.

"Isn't he married?"

"I don't think so," said Fliss. "Why?"

"He could go out with Brown Owl," Rosie suggested.

"What a brilliant idea!" said Fliss "Why didn't I think of that?"

"Probably because I thought of it first," I said.

"It was my idea," Kenny muttered.

"Rosie thought of it, actually," said Fliss.

"How would you know?" I said. "You were asleep, *actually*!"

Things could have got difficult. Me and Fliss often get into arguments about who thought of something first, but then my mum called us for breakfast so that was that.

But whoever's idea it was, it spelled t-r-o-u-b-l-e. And we'd have been better off if nobody had thought of it. But you know Fliss, once she gets hold of an idea she won't let go, especially if it's got anything to do with weddings.

"Just think," she said, "they might fall in love and get married. I bet Brown Owl would be so grateful, she'd even let us be her bridesmaids."

"I doubt it," I said.

Kenny rolled her eyes. She doesn't mind dressing up for a laugh, but she wouldn't want to be a bridesmaid. Personally, I wouldn't mind, if I could choose what I wore. I'm really into silver. I've got a pair of silver shoes and occasionally, at weekends, I'm allowed to wear silver nail varnish. The others sometimes call me Spaceman. But I couldn't see Brown Owl wanting bridesmaids dressed in silver.

I said, "Knowing Brown Owl, she'd probably make us wear our Brownie uniforms."

"But we'd still get to go to her wedding," said Fliss.

"I think it's a great idea," said Lyndz. "It'd be nice for both of them."

"Come on, let's make a plan," said Felicity.

"I think we'd better find out if he's already got a girlfriend first," I said.

"How will we do that?" said Rosie.

"We'll ask him," said Kenny.

"When?"

"On Monday," I said. "The sooner the better."

CHAPTER FOUR

We all go to the same school. It's called Cuddington County Primary and it's a great school. Our teacher's called Mrs Weaver and she's great too, so's the Head, Mrs Poole. She never shouts, she just looks disappointed with you, if you get sent to her. It's not so bad, as long as you keep looking at your feet.

There's only one thing wrong with our school and that's Mrs Pickett; she's one of the dinner ladies. Mrs Pickernose, we call her. She does nothing but tell people off. She is bad news. But apart from her, we all like our school.

Dishy Dave is what we call Mr Driver. That's because he's dead tall and good-looking, a bit like Brad Pitt. And he's a good laugh. He calls us 'guys' and the boys 'girls'. He kicks a football around with them sometimes and he plays the piano for us to dance to; he knows all sorts of tunes.

Practising our dance routines is one of our best skives. We go into the studio and turn all the lights off, apart from one or two spots, and pretend we're dancers with Oasis. Or sometimes we go in the hall to dance and Mr Driver plays the piano. If the M&Ms haven't got there first, that is. The M&Ms are our biggest enemies – Emma Hughes and Emily Berryman, yuk! – but I'll tell you about them another time.

Mr Driver lives just down the road from school and he's always in and out. The only time he's too busy to talk to you is at home time, when he has to get on with the cleaning, but apart from that he never minds a good old chat.

So, on Monday, we went looking for him at break time. We found him cleaning some graffiti off the side of one of the mobile classrooms. We sidled up to him and then hung around waiting for the right moment.

"Uh-oh," he said, "here comes trouble." But he smiled and went on scrubbing. "This wasn't your handiwork, I suppose?"

"Nooo!" we said. "Certainly not!" And we all looked as if butter wouldn't melt in our mouths, as my grandma says.

After a bit I said, "Dave…" He doesn't mind us calling him Dave.

"Have you got a girlfriend?"

He stopped scrubbing and started to grin. "No. But I think I'm a bit old for you, don't you?"

I went bright red. The others started to laugh as if it was *so* funny.

"She didn't mean that," said Fliss. "We

were just interested. Have you really not got a girlfriend?"

"Nope," he said.

"Would you like one?" said Lyndz.

"Nope," he said. "Too much trouble."

"No, seriously," said Kenny.

Mr Driver sort of narrowed his eyes at us. "Why are you asking?"

"We could find you one, if you like," I said.

"What's the catch?"

We all said, "There is no catch."

"In that case I'd like Pamela Anderson."

"Don't be silly," said Fliss. "We don't know Pamela Anderson."

"Sorry, not interested, then," he said. "I'm saving myself for Pamela."

And he went back to scrubbing *Wiggie woz here* off the back of the mobile. Then the whistle went for the end of break. We shrugged and sort of drifted off.

"Do you think he was serious?" said Felicity.

"Oh, get a life," I said.

"Course he wasn't serious," said Lyndz.

"Where's he ever going to meet Pamela Anderson?" said Kenny.

"Even so," I said, not feeling very hopeful, "I doubt if he's going to settle for Brown Owl."

I wasn't being horrible about Brown Owl. She's very nice. She's quite pretty, with dark eyes and shoulder-length brown hair, and she looks really smart in her uniform. But Pamela Anderson she is not. She works in Barclays Bank and sometimes when I go in with my mum she's behind the counter and she smiles at us. She wears glasses at work and they really suit her but she doesn't wear them all the time. She's got a nice smile and a good sense of humour. Or she had. But she looks like a real wet weekend these days. It wasn't only Lyndsey who felt sorry for her, we all did.

But feeling sorry wasn't enough. We needed action, and action was our speciality! We decided to call it Operation Blind Date, or OBD for short. That was Felicity's idea! She even wanted us to write to Cilla Black to get Dave and Brown Owl on the show, but fortunately that was one of Fliss's bright ideas we decided against.

CHAPTER FIVE

Hang on a minute. Was that the phone? Quick, let's go and listen at the top of the stairs. Careful, my door squeaks. If my mum hears us, I'm in real doom.

"Hello... No, Felicity, you can't talk to Francesca... no, I'm sorry, she can't call you back... because Francesca is grounded... I haven't decided how long for. Possibly for ever...

"Yes, I'll tell her you rang..."

Uh-oh. If my mum's calling me Francesca, it must be serious. I wish I knew what Brown Owl's been saying. Do you suppose she's told them about Kenny and Rosie and the shopping-trolley incident? Or even worse, she might have told them about the letter. Which letter? The letter we sent Dishy Dave from Brown Owl, of course. That was *definitely not* my idea. I knew from the beginning *that* was a mistake.

But the problem was, we needed to get Dave and Brown Owl together and it wasn't going to be easy. As far as we knew they'd never even set eyes on each other. But we had to start somewhere, so we decided to start with Dave.

Every time he saw us around school he kept on asking us if there was any word from Pamela yet, and telling us he was keeping Saturday free, and other silly things. So we decided we'd tell him about this person we knew, this grown-up friend of ours called Madeline, who really wanted to meet him.

We didn't tell him she was our Brown Owl. As Kenny said, someone who wants to go out with Pamela Anderson might not be interested if he knows she runs the Brownies.

"So, what's this *friend* like?" he asked.

"Nice," we all said in chorus.

He rolled his eyes. "What does she do?"

"She works in a bank," said Felicity. That seemed OK.

"How old is she?"

"About your age," said Kenny, quick as a flash. Dave didn't look convinced.

"She's got her own car," I said. He seemed impressed by that.

Then he asked us what she looked like. OK, so perhaps we exaggerated a bit, but like my grandma says, beauty is in the eye of the beholder.

We got stuck when he asked us what music she was into. We hadn't a clue.

"Blur, Oasis, I think," said Felicity. Even I knew that was a mistake.

"That's kids' stuff," said Dave, pulling a face.

"No, she's got it wrong," said Kenny. "I think she likes... classical music."

He pulled an even worse face.

"It could be country and western," I said. His face lit up.

"That's right. It *was* country and western," said Kenny. "I remember now."

"At least she's got good taste in music," said Dave. We all nodded enthusiastically.

By now Dave was looking seriously interested, but the whistle had gone for lessons. We headed back to the classroom.

Felicity said, "I didn't know Brown Owl liked country and western."

Honestly, what is she like? She can be so dozy sometimes.

But we knew Dave was interested because after that he stopped mentioning Pamela Anderson every time he saw us and started asking how Madeline was. Felicity was so convinced we'd got it sorted that she started doing little drawings of what kind of bridesmaid's dresses we would all wear.

"Look, don't bank on it," I said. "We still haven't talked to Brown Owl."

That night it was Brownies. Our Brownie pack meets in the church hall on a Thursday night. It's not a very big pack but there are four sixes. Me and Kenny and Fliss are all sixers. Lyndz is my seconder and Rosie has joined Kenny's six. At the moment we're all working on our Brownie Highway. It's the last of our Brownie journeys. Some of us are nearly old enough to leave Brownies. We're writing a play and making puppets with Snowy Owl. We're supposed to be doing a puppet show for our mums and dads, but it's taken us weeks just to make the puppets.

We were all sitting round a table and Brown Owl came over to see how we were getting on. She sat down with us, so I grabbed the opportunity. I pretended to be dead laid back.

"Brown Owl, what kind of music d'you like?"

"All sorts," she said.

"But what's your favourite?"

She shrugged. "Jazz… opera…"

"Opera?" I said.

"Don't you like Oasis?" said Lyndz.

"I've never heard them," said Brown Owl. Lyndsey's jaw dropped.

"What about country and western?" said Kenny, desperately.

"Yes, it's OK. I like all sorts."

We let out a sigh of relief.

"Brown Owl, how old are you?" Felicity asked.

"Felicity!" said Snowy Owl, shocked.

"Never you mind," said Brown Owl, smiling. "It's not polite to ask a lady her age."

Fliss said, "Sorry."

"I should think so too," said Snowy Owl.

Why are grown-ups so funny about their

age? I don't get it. But at least it had made Brown Owl smile. Then Rosie went too far.

"Brown Owl, have you got a boyfriend?"

Brown Owl's face went all serious and stern-looking and she got up and walked off. "You just concentrate on your puppets," she told us, "instead of my love-life."

"What did you have to go and say that for?" I hissed at Rosie.

"How else are we going to find out?" she hissed back.

Snowy Owl looked at us suspiciously.

"We were only wondering," I said, trying to look innocent. "She just doesn't seem very happy."

Snowy looked over to make sure Brown Owl couldn't hear her.

"She hasn't got a boyfriend," she whispered. "And it's time she had. No one's worth getting yourself that miserable over. I've told her that, but she's not ready to hear it yet. So don't you lot go upsetting her any more, d'you hear?"

We all nodded and looked at one another, but we didn't say anything else to Snowy Owl. We just got on with painting our puppet heads. You can't tell with grown-ups who you can trust and who you can't. But at least one thing was clear, Brown Owl needed our help, even if she didn't know it yet.

CHAPTER SIX

We thought we'd at least got Dave on our side. So it was a bit of a surprise that on Friday, when we mentioned it, he burst out laughing.

"Are you still on about that?" he said. "Don't you think that joke's wearing a bit thin?"

"But it's not a joke," said Kenny.

"We're deadly serious," I said.

"Deadly?" said Dave. "That sounds pretty serious. Come on, guys, you're in my way." And then we had to move because he wanted to start polishing the hall floor.

Fliss had one last go. "What would we have to do to convince you?" she asked him.

"Get me a photo." A photo, I thought, where are we going to get that? "Or, better still, get her to send me a letter," he said, smiling.

A photo was bad enough, but a letter was completely out of the question. Or I thought it was, until on the way home from school, Lyndz had one of her crackpot ideas.

"*We* could write one," she said.

"We'd never get away with it," I said. "He'd know it was our writing."

I'm the only one who can do joined-up handwriting that doesn't look like a bowl of spaghetti. But nobody would believe it belonged to a grown-up who works in a bank.

"We don't need to *write* it," said Kenny.

"We can print it on the computer. And it's dead easy to fake a signature. I copy my dad's all the time."

"Oh, really?" I said, raising one eyebrow. I'm the only one who can do that trick, too.

Kenny grinned. "Just the odd cheque when my pocket money runs out."

"Honestly?" said Felicity, who'd believe anything you told her.

"She's joking," I said, tapping the side of my head. "Derrr!"

"It's just a game," said Kenny. "I've got this really ancient prescription pad my dad gave me. I sign them Doctor *McKenzie*. It looks dead cool."

"But what would we put in the letter?" I said. I still didn't like the idea.

"You are a handsome hunk. I lurv you," said Lyndz, rolling her eyes and then collapsing in a fit of giggles.

"We were born to be together." Kenny clutched her heart and puckered her lips.

After that the pair of them just went a bit haywire. Kenny started doing a terrible French accent and Lyndz kept fluttering her eyelashes.

"All right, calm down, you dodos," I said, but none of us could stop laughing. People were staring at us across the street. It was really wicked.

But I remember thinking of what my grandma says, when things get out of hand: "You mark my words, this'll all end in tears."

It was right in the middle of all this that we found out a bit more about Rosie's family. We often walk past her house on our way home from school and hope she'll invite us in, but so far no such luck. I know some people's parents are dead strict and don't like other kids in their house. Thank goodness mine aren't like that – but neither was her mum. She often said, "Rosie, don't keep your friends on the step. Ask them in." But she wouldn't and we couldn't work out why.

We knew her dad didn't live with them, she'd told us that, but then lots of people in our class haven't got a dad at home.

Fliss hasn't. She's got Andy, her mum's boyfriend, but he's not her dad. Her proper dad lives in the next street with his girlfriend Maria and the new baby, Posie. Fliss and her brother go round every Friday to her dad's for tea, but they don't live with him.

Also, Rosie had told us about her brother Adam. We hadn't seen him yet because he goes to a special school. We knew he used a wheelchair; we'd seen it in the back of her mum's car. But Rosie said he couldn't talk either, so we thought perhaps she didn't want us to go to her house because of Adam. But we were wrong about that too.

I had to go and put my foot in it, didn't I? Me and my big mouth!

We were leaning on Rosie's gate; I said, "It's Friday today, if we had a sleepover tonight we could write the letter and take it to Dave's tomorrow."

"Wicked!" said Fliss. "And we could make all our plans for OBD."

I kept staring at Rosie's house, hoping she would take the hint, but she didn't.

"Well, we can't have it at mine," said Fliss. "My mum still hasn't got over the bubble-bath episode." Some time I'll tell you that story!

"Don't look at me," said Lyndz. "My mum and dad are decorating, *again*!" Lyndz's mum and dad are always doing something to her house. Extending it or decorating it or taking it apart and putting it back together again.

"I suppose I could ask mine," Kenny offered. "But Monster-features will only interfere." Kenny has the worst sister the human imagination could conjure up. We call her *Molly the Monster*. And poor old

Kenny has to share a bedroom with her!

We'd already had the one last week at mine, so that left just one person and I was getting tired of dropping hints.

"What about at yours?" I said to Rosie, straight out, just like that. But the minute I'd said it, I wished I hadn't. Rosie went bright red and shook her head.

"Why not?" I said.

"Because," said Rosie, starting to look as if she might cry.

"Look, if it's because of Adam..." I started, without knowing how I was going to finish.

"We don't mind, honest," said Fliss.

"No," said Lyndz. "I've got an uncle in a wheelchair."

"So?" said Rosie. "What about it? This is nothing to do with Adam, you stupids. It's the state my house is in." And then she burst into tears.

She told us her dad was a builder. He'd bought the house to do up, but he'd met his girlfriend soon after they'd moved in. Now he'd gone off and left them in this amazing big house which Rosie said was a complete tip.

"He says he'll fix it, but he never does. It's horrible! There's hardly any carpets. My bedroom's got no paper on the walls."

"We don't care about wallpaper," I said, trying to make her feel better.

"Well, I do," she said, going through her gate and slamming it behind her. "It's not fair. I hate everybody!" And she went up her path, sobbing.

All the others were looking at me as if to say, "Well, I hope you're satisfied now."

But I wasn't. I felt terrible. I hadn't meant to make her cry. I went straight home and asked my mum if we could *please* have another sleepover at my house. I even got down on my knees into my famous begging pose.

"Pretty please," I said, "with cherries on the top."

My mum looked down at me pretending to be a well-trained dog, and shook her head. "I don't know what makes you think that performance is likely to persuade anyone," she said.

But it did. I got straight on the phone and rang round.

"It's on for tonight! Sleepover, at mine. Seven o'clock."

"You're wonderful," I told my mum. "I'm your slave for ever. Whatever you desire, command and I will obey."

My mum just grinned and kept on watching the news, but my dad said, "Right, that's two cups of tea now and extra washing-up for a week."

"It's a deal," I said. "You're the best." Thank goodness for groovy parents!

CHAPTER SEVEN

I think they started to get suspicious that night when we were so keen to go to bed early. Usually I have to beg and plead with them to stay up late on a Friday for *Friends*. It's my best programme! Coo-el. But there we go. Sometimes there are more important things even than *Friends*! So by eight o'clock we were all in our jimjams in my bedroom, talking really quietly.

Kenny and I were sharing a bed again, Lyndz and Felicity had got the bunks and Rosie was on the camp bed this time. She was looking like a wet weekend again, even though nobody had mentioned her outburst at the gate. It felt funny, because we were all thinking about it, even though we weren't saying anything, if you see what I mean. It was as though there was an elephant standing in the corner but no one was mentioning the fact.

"Right, let's get started," said old bossy-boots Fliss. "Who's doing the typing?"

I can tell you now what she'll be when she grows up: a teacher! She's always practising bossing us about.

"I'll do it," I said, turning my computer on. The others all crowded round me. "Right, I'm ready," I said.

Then we all sat there looking at the blank screen.

"Dear Dave..." said Felicity. Then she sat there looking very pleased with herself.

"Oh, good start," I said. "Well, that's the

hard bit over."

"'I really fancy you,'" said Kenny. "'How about going out with me?'"

"That is so sad," I said.

Rosie shook her head. "Brown Owl definitely wouldn't say that."

"So what would she say, clever clogs?" said Kenny.

"Something like: 'I've seen you around school; you look like a nice person.'"

"You look like a *nice person*," said Kenny in a whiny voice. "That's so naff. Where's the romance in that?"

"There's no *lurv* in that," agreed Lyndsey, getting all giggly. I could just see them starting each other off again.

"Listen! Listen," I said. "Rosie's right. It doesn't have to be sloppy stuff. I'll write down what she just said."

"Then say something about how she likes country and western music," said Rosie.

"Oh, yes," said Fliss. "That's important,

Frankie. Don't forget that bit."

"Yeah, yeah. I've put that. Then what?"

"Put: 'I'd like to go out with you. How about it?'" said Kenny.

I wrote: '*I'd like to go out with you.*' Brown Owl wouldn't say "how about it"!

"Anything else?"

"That's enough, isn't it?" said Rosie.

"Don't we want to say where they could meet?"

"The bus station."

"Outside the chippie."

"The park gates."

"Put: 'I'll be wearing a red carnation'," said Kenny.

It was like a story we were making up. We could have put anything. Dave might turn up, but there was one bit we still hadn't worked out.

"How on earth are we going to get Brown Owl there?"

"We'll just choose a place where we know Brown Owl's going to be," said

Kenny, as if that was the easiest thing in the world.

"Not at Brownies. She won't want him turning up there," said Fliss.

"Or in the bank," I said.

"Or at her house, I guess," said Lyndz.

"Where else does she go?" asked Rosie.

"She shops on a Saturday at the SavaCentre. I always see her when I go with my mum," said Felicity.

"Oh, how *romantic*!" said Kenny.

"Meet me by the frozen peas," said Lyndz.

"We can cuddle by the cabbages," said Kenny. They can be so silly.

"D'you think she'll be there tomorrow?" said Rosie, ignoring them.

"Probs," said Felicity.

"Tomorrow's no good, I've got badminton," said Kenny.

"Not in the afternoon, you haven't," I said.

"D'you think you could get your mum

and dad to take us?" said Fliss.

"All of us?"

"Yes. We all need to be there."

"Tell them it's for a project we're doing at school," said Kenny.

Well, that was almost true, wasn't it? I just wouldn't tell them the project was called Operation Blind Date. And it *was* in a good cause.

I finished the letter off: *I'll be shopping in the SavaCentre on Saturday afternoon. I'll see you there.*

"How shall I sign it?"

"'Lots of love and kisses,'" said Kenny, getting really stupid.

"'Yours affectionately, Madeline,'" suggested Fliss.

But none of us could spell "affectionately" so we just put: *Love from…* Then I printed it off and Kenny signed it with a huge scribble.

"What's that supposed to say?"

"Madeline."

"You can't read it."

"You're not supposed to be able to read it," said Kenny. "That's what signatures are like."

"He can read the letter, that's the important thing," Lyndz agreed.

"When are we going to give it to him?" said Rosie.

"We'll have to take it round in the morning," I said.

"I can't," said Kenny. "Badminton."

"I've got to look after Spike," said Lyndz. That's her baby brother. "But I can come back after dinner."

"OK," I said. "That means *we'll* have to take it," I told Fliss and Rosie. "We can take Pepsi for a walk past his house."

By now, my mum was coming in to see if we wanted drinks and biscuits. I knew we'd been far too quiet and she was looking suspicious. So we had our usual silly half-hour before we got into bed. You know the kind of thing: three rounds of International Gladiators, which as usual ended up with Lyndz having one of her fits of hiccups.

"OK. Lights out," said Dad. "Nighty-night. Don't let the werewolves bite."

"It's bedbugs," said Felicity, giggling.

"Not in this h-o-u-s-e," my dad howled. Sometimes parents can be so embarrassing!

After he'd gone down and we were lying in the dark, Rosie said, "Thanks for inviting me again, even though I told you I couldn't have you round at my house."

"It's OK," said Lyndsey. "We don't mind, do we?"

"No," said the others. "It's not your fault."

In a way I didn't mind either. Rosie was sort of growing on me. She had some good ideas and she could be quite a laugh, but there was a principle here.

My mum and dad are both lawyers and

they're always telling me about principles. If you agree to something, you should stick to it. Like if I say, OK, I'll set the table every night or wash up on Mondays and Wednesdays, then I should do it. Or if I don't like my dad interrupting me when I'm watching *Home and Away*, I shouldn't barge in on him when he's watching the news. So if we want to be in a Sleepover Club and sleep at other people's houses, then it's only right that we let everyone sleep at our house. That's fair, isn't it?

So I said, "But I still don't see why we can't sleep at yours, if your mum'll let us."

"Oh, Frankie," the others started up. "She's already told us why."

"Just because her bedroom's in a tip? She's not seen Kenny's yet."

"Thanks a bunch," said Kenny.

I said, "You know what I mean." Kenny's famous for how untidy she is. It drives her sister barmy.

"Well, it wouldn't bother me whether there was paper on the walls," Kenny agreed.

"Nor me," said Lyndsey, "as long as we have a laugh."

At first Rosie still didn't say anything, but after a bit she said, "Well, OK, if you're sure. I'll see what my mum says."

I thought, two-one, yeah! But I didn't say anything and neither did anyone else. In fact, the silence got a bit creepy, so we were all relieved when Fliss said, "Isn't it time for our midnight feast?"

"Yeah," I said. "Let's see what we've got tonight. Oh, brillo, rhubarb and apple fizzers!"

CHAPTER EIGHT

Next morning, as soon as I woke up, I went into mum and dad's room. They were already awake, sitting up in bed, as usual on a Saturday, reading the papers.

"Anyone like a cuppa?"

"We've got one, thanks," said Dad. "Pity you weren't up ten minutes earlier."

"But you can let Pepsi out," said Mum.

"No problem," I said. "I'll take her for a nice long walk later. Anything else? Breakfast in bed? Bowl of cereal? Piece of toast? Bacon butty?"

I think I must have been overdoing it,

because they both looked at me over the top of their glasses.

"What are you after?" said Mum.

"Nothing," I said, as if butter wouldn't melt in my mouth. "Just trying to be helpful."

"Francesca? What's going on?"

"What are you after?"

"I was just wondering if you'd like to take us with you to the supermarket."

"All five of you?" said Mum.

"Why would I?" said Dad.

"It would save time. We could help you."

"I think not," said Dad. "I suspect it would take me five times as long."

"Oh, please, Dad. It's really important. It's for a project for school. We need some information on... prices."

"Well, that's different," said Dad.

"Why didn't you say that in the first place?" said Mum. "It's always the best policy to start with the truth. You're much more likely to get what you want that way."

Well, that made me feel really lousy. I hate fibbing to my parents. It always makes me feel horrible. My mum's right: if I ask for something straight out, they usually say yes. But this time was different. I just knew, if I told them the whole story, they wouldn't understand. So what else could I do?

When I got back in my bedroom, I should have guessed it was too quiet to be true. The others suddenly all yanked back their covers and hurled their pillows at me.

"Pack it in!" I yelled. "That's the last time I do you lot a favour." I was sitting on the floor, surrounded by pillows.

"What did they say?" asked Kenny.

"They said yes, of course," I said.

"Wicked!"

"One-nil," said Kenny.

"Frankie's the greatest," said Lyndz.

"Humph," I said, grumpily. And I didn't cheer up until they'd all grovelled at my feet and called me a star. "That's more like it," I said.

After breakfast Kenny's mum came and collected her to take her to badminton and she took Lyndsey home at the same time.

"Is it all right if they come back this afternoon," I said, "to go to the supermarket?"

"We're doing this shopping project at school and we've got to collect some information," said Kenny.

"Comparing prices," said Fliss.

"Which are the cheapest brands," said Lyndz.

Suddenly this little white lie had turned into a complete story. I was almost beginning to believe it myself.

Fliss and Rosie and I walked Pepsi along

the road I usually take to school. The letter was burning a hole in my pocket. I couldn't wait to get rid of it. I was feeling pretty nervous, but I didn't say anything because by now Fliss was really starting to panic. She kept stopping in the middle of the pavement and gasping.

"What if he isn't in?" she said.

"We'll post it through the letterbox," said Rosie.

"That's what you do with letters," I reminded her.

We walked on a bit further, then she stopped again.

"But then how will we know he's got it? What if he doesn't open it before this afternoon? What if he's out? What if he's ill? What if he's gone on holiday?"

"What if he's been abducted by aliens?" I suggested.

"What if he's turned overnight into a dog?" said Rosie.

"A dog?" said Fliss, frowning.

"Joke," I said. "It was a joke."

"Well, I don't think it was very funny," said Fliss.

But me and Rosie did. We really cracked up.

When we got close to Dave's house, we all completely lost our nerve. I wasn't absolutely sure I knew which house was his. It's a road where all the houses look the same. Fliss insisted it was number 37, the one with a green front door, but I had a feeling it was the one two doors down with a black front door.

We stood across the road hoping he'd come out or appear at the window. But he didn't. After five minutes, by which time I was convinced everyone in the road was watching us behind their curtains, or, worse still, phoning the police, I suddenly remembered something.

"Dave doesn't have a car," I said. There was a car in the drive of number 37.

"It could be a visitor's," Fliss pointed

out. She hates to lose an argument.

So Rosie said, "Why don't we just knock on the door and ask?"

"I'm not," said Fliss.

"I'd better not. I've got the dog," I said. "She might growl at him." The other two looked at me. Pepsi hardly ever growls. She's the softest dog on four legs.

"Oh, I'll go," said Rosie. Just like that. She held her hand out for the letter and then marched straight over. She knocked on the door and waited. She looked over her shoulder and smiled. We waved to her. We were seriously impressed.

But nothing happened. So she knocked again, and waited what seemed like ages. This time when she looked back at us she wasn't smiling. Then she must have heard someone coming because she just dropped the letter on the step and ran. So we ran as well, right down the road, as if Dracula had come to the door.

But when we'd got far enough away, I

stopped and let myself look back. Dave was standing at the door in his pyjamas, shaking his head and grinning. So I waved to him, then I ran to catch up with the others. Now at least we knew he'd got it.

CHAPTER NINE

On the way to the supermarket, I sat by Dad in the front seat and the others piled into the back of the estate. Dad looked over his shoulder.

"You don't seem to have much with you. Don't you need little clipboards or something?"

"It's all right," I said, waving my notebook. "I'll write it all down. They can copy off me on Monday."

"Very public-spirited," said Dad.

When we got into the store, Dad told us. "Now, no one is to set foot outside the store without me. It's quite busy, so try not to get in anyone's way. Meet me at the checkouts in one hour. Who's got a watch?"

We all put up our hands, just as if we were at school.

"OK," I said. "Synchronise watches."

Dad said, "I make it 2.05 precisely."

Lyndz stared at her watch. "Does that mean the long hand's before or after the two?"

"After!" said Kenny.

"Honestly, Lyndz," I said. "Are you ever going to learn to tell the time?"

"It's not my fault. It's this watch."

She certainly would have got on better if she'd had a digital like the rest of us, but Lyndz has a real mental block about telling the time anyway. She always says, "Why does it matter?"

Dad laughed and went off. "Remember, no mischief! I don't want to have to pay for any breakages. Do you understand?"

We all nodded and smiled. Yes, yes, we understood. Famous last words.

We decided to split up and take an aisle each, to see if there was any sign of Brown Owl or Dave. I got Pet Foods and Toiletries. I couldn't believe how many people there were shopping that afternoon, and most of them seemed to be buying dog biscuits and shampoo. We kept waving to each other and shaking our heads, then going back up the aisle we'd come down, in case we'd missed them.

After about a quarter of an hour I tried to round the others up, but every time I got to the bottom of an aisle I'd see them disappearing back up it. I was nearly tearing my hair out. Now I knew what it was like being a mum in charge of four naughty kids.

"Right, let's try and stay together," I said.

"Yes, Mum," said Kenny, grinning.

We saw plenty of other people from school or Brownies with their mums, but no Brown Owl. In fact, we bumped into Felicity's Auntie Jill. You know, Snowy Owl.

"What are you doing here?" she asked Fliss.

"Helping Frankie's dad," she said, looking a bit guilty.

"He must be doing a big shop to need five helpers."

"Have you seen Brown Owl anywhere?" I asked.

"She was parking her car in the car park as I drove in. Why?"

"No reason," said Fliss.

"We've got a message for her, that's all," said Rosie.

"From my mum," I added hurriedly.

"Well, she'll be in here somewhere. Now, don't get into any trouble," she warned Fliss. "You do exactly what Mr

Thomas tells you."

While we'd been talking to Snowy Owl, Kenny and Lyndsey had wandered off.

"Where have they gone?" I asked Rosie.

"Search me," she said.

"Well, let's try and find them. Then we've got to stay together."

Brown Owl was obviously around and it was just a matter of time before we found her. We hadn't seen Dave yet. We just had to hope he'd turn up. But we couldn't find Kenny and Lyndz anywhere and I was getting really worried.

What I didn't say, but I was certainly thinking, was that sometimes, when those two get together, they go completely haywire. I just hoped this wasn't one of those times. But, then, as we stood at one end of the Wine and Beer aisle, I saw something at the other end that told me it *was* one of those times.

Lyndz was racing round with a full

supermarket trolley, which would have been bad enough. What made it worse was that it was full of Kenny.

We set off as fast as we could to follow them. But we'd hardly gone a few steps when we stopped dead. Coming down the aisle towards us was Dave.

He looked really different. We'd never seen him except in his overalls or work clothes. He looked even nicer than he did at school. He did look really dishy. He'd got a leather jacket on and jeans and black leather boots. He was carrying a basket but all he'd got in it so far were a couple of tins.

We stood there, sort of hidden by a family with a full shopping trolley, not sure whether to rush up and say hello or go back the way we'd come. Behind him, just coming round the corner, we spotted Brown Owl. That made our minds up for us. Fortunately neither of them had seen us yet.

"Quick," I said. "This way." And I led Fliss and Rosie backwards up the aisle.

"Wasn't that Dave?" Fliss almost squealed, craning her neck to see him. I grabbed her by the arm and pulled her back.

"Yes," I said through gritted teeth. "Now, tell me something I don't know."

"Wasn't that Brown Owl as well?" said Rosie.

"Yes, it was, but more important right now, where are Kenny and Lyndz?"

Suddenly we heard a noise from the next aisle which sort of answered the question.

It wasn't exactly a crash. It would have been, if they'd been glass bottles. But this sounded more like skittles being knocked over. About two hundred of them. It was a whole display of plastic bottles of mineral water. They landed with a dull thud and then rolled in all directions.

I knew straight away who'd run into them. You didn't have to be Mastermind to work that out. This was a big store. I just hoped my dad was right at the other end of it.

CHAPTER TEN

As we turned the corner, there were people picking up bottles in every direction. Kenny and Lyndz, with faces the colour of bottled beetroot, were in the middle, trying to put the display back together again. One or two of the bottles had exploded and there was a fizzy river running down the aisle. A worried-looking boy came with a mop.

My brain felt as if it was about to explode too. I was thinking about Dave and Brown Owl in the next aisle and wondering whether they'd suddenly appear and walk straight into it all. Even worse, I was dreading my dad coming round the corner and finding us.

Fliss and Rosie and I rushed over to help collect up the bottles, but by now the manager had arrived. That's put the king in the cake, I thought, now we're going to get it. But all he was bothered about was getting the mess cleared up. He didn't seem to care how it had happened. He took the bottles off us and sort of shooed us away. So we all ran off before he changed his mind.

"You pair are too lucky to live," I said.

"It wasn't our fault, was it?" Kenny said to Lyndz. "It was an accident." But then they gave themselves away by giggling.

"Come on," I said. "They're over here." I pointed down the next aisle. And there they were – gone.

"This way," I said, "follow me! And stick together."

At the end of each aisle we peered

round the corner shelves until we found them.

Brown Owl was reading the ingredients on a jar of pasta sauce. Dave was having a conversation with a five-year-old I recognised from school and his mum and grandma. But then he turned our way and walked towards us... and towards Brown Owl.

"Quick!" I said. And we all squeezed behind a stack of baked beans. "Anybody knock these over," I warned them, "and you're dead."

Dave had stopped beside Brown Owl and was waiting for her to move so that he could reach a jar of pasta sauce for himself.

"Don't they make a nice couple?" whispered Fliss.

"They like the same pasta sauce," whispered Rosie.

"Ahhh, that's nice," said Lyndz.

"So a-romantic!" said Kenny in a stupid

Italian accent.

"Shhh!" I said, terrified they'd hear and look over and see us watching them.

Brown Owl suddenly realised she was in Dave's way and smiled at him and moved along until she was out of his way and then stopped to check her list. She'd got a full trolley and she was crossing a lot off. It looked as if she was just about finished. This could be our last chance.

"What are we going to do?" said Fliss.

"I don't know," I said.

Dave was coming straight towards us. So Kenny and I popped up and waved to him, then we both pointed at Brown Owl.

Dave stopped and frowned, but we kept on pointing until he turned and looked back over his shoulder. When he saw Brown Owl, he looked at us with his head on one side and then he pointed at her as well. We all popped up and nodded.

Dave smiled and headed back towards her. We weren't close enough to hear what he said but we'd all got our fingers and toes crossed. I don't know about the others but I was too nervous to breathe.

Brown Owl was looking very surprised. Dave looked as if he was telling her a joke, but she didn't seem to be getting it. She just kept on frowning until suddenly the penny seemed to drop. Dave nodded in our direction and Brown Owl looked over too.

We all ducked down but I think she saw us. Then she started to shake her head as if she couldn't believe what he was telling her. They'd *been* talking quietly, but we heard the next thing loud and clear.

"I'm *not* looking for a boyfriend. What letter? I didn't write any letter."

And then the worst thing of all happened. Dave took out the letter and showed it to her. When Brown Owl read it, she sort of erupted and went into orbit.

We didn't wait around to find out what happened next, because I suddenly remembered my dad and realised what time it was.

"It's gone quarter past three," I shrieked. "Come on!" I raced off, with the others dodging shopping trolleys behind me. When we reached the checkout, Dad was standing there with his mad-as-a-hatter face on.

I raised my hands. "Dad, we're really, truly, genuinely, totally, completely sorry."

"We got lost," said Kenny.

"Carried away," said Fliss.

"Forgot the time," said Lyndz.

"Just spare me the excuses," said Dad, already halfway out of the door.

We raced after him, hardly daring to look back in case Brown Owl was following us. We helped Dad lift the shopping into the back of the car in record time. Then we jumped in the car and kept our heads down. Nobody spoke all the way home and on the way back

Dad dropped the others off.

Kenny was last to be dropped off. As we drove away, she gave me a good-luck sign. I had a feeling I was going to need it – and I was right, wasn't I?

GOODBYE

So now you know the whole story. We had no idea it would turn out like this. We were just trying to be helpful. Grounded, my mum said. And it wasn't even my fault. Well, there we go. Like my grandma says, life's very unfair.

I wish I was a fly on the wall in our lounge right now. I'd love to hear Brown Owl's side of the story. But then again, perhaps I wouldn't.

It seems a real shame; she and Dishy Dave made such a nice couple.

Uh-oh. What was that? I think it was the front door closing. Quick, let's look out the window, but don't let her see you, whatever you do. That's Brown Owl all right. Thank goodness she's gone. If she's told them everything, I'm not worth a life.

"Francesca! Please come down here, *this minute*."

Uh-oh. This could be the end. The end of the Sleepover Club. Possibly the end of Francesca Theresa Thomas. Well, say a prayer for me.

Goodbye. Farewell. Au revoir (that's French, in case you don't know). Arrivederci (that's Italian).

I bet you're impressed. I can say hello and goodbye in five different languages. My grandad taught me the last time I went to stay. Now, what was it in Spanish...?

"Francesca! I mean **now**!"

"Coming, Mum!"

I'd better go. Keep your fingers crossed for me. See ya!

The Sleepover Club at Felicity's

Join the Sleepover Club: Frankie, Kenny, Felicity, Rosie and Lyndsey, five girls who just want to have fun – but who always end up in mischief.

A sleepover isn't a sleepover without a midnight feast and when the food runs out and everyone's still hungry, the Sleepover Club tiptoe down to the kitchen. But – quick! – the toaster's on fire!

Pack up your sleepover kit and drop in on the fun!

0 00 675236 5